THE NO GLAM SHOW

KANIKA BHATIA TOMAR

Made with ❤ on the Notion Press Platform
www.notionpress.com

To all whose names find a place in these pages—
Thank you for the moments, the meaning,
and the memories that made this story whole.

And to Aelika and Rahul—
the anchors of my journey,
your steadfast love and silent strength
carried me through shadow and shine.
This book lives because you believed.

Contents

Foreword

"The No Glam Show" is not just a novel—it's a mirror held up to the quiet truths we often live but rarely speak aloud. With unflinching honesty and poetic grace, Kanika Bhatia Tomar unravels the life of Kiara, a girl born into tradition but destined to question it all.

What struck me most as an early reader was how Kanika breathes life into everyday emotions—joy, loss, love, and rebellion—without ever needing spectacle. Her prose is subtle, her characters deeply human, and her voice, entirely her own. Through Kiara's story, she offers us a window into the complexities of growing up female in a world where expectations often speak louder than dreams.

This book does not shout for attention—it earns it, sentence by sentence. Whether you come for the nostalgia, the family drama, or the quiet strength of a young girl learning to live on her own terms, The No Glam Show will stay with you long after the final page.

It's a rare thing to read a debut that feels this grounded and this true.

— Vandana Soni
Early Reader

Preface

The No Glam Show began as a whisper—an idea that lingered quietly in my mind for years, waiting for the right moment to be heard. It's not a story of perfection, but of the raw, unfiltered moments that shape us. It's about the silences we grow up with, the questions we're afraid to ask, and the quiet rebellions that define who we become.

Kiara's journey is fictional, but her emotions are not. She is built from fragments of reality—stories I've heard, lived, or imagined late at night when the world felt too loud. Writing her story was, in many ways, a return to my own roots, to the complexity of family, to the contradictions of being raised in a culture that both nurtures and confines.

This book is a tribute to every girl who has ever felt unseen, every woman who has learned to reclaim her space, and every person navigating life between expectation and selfhood.

I didn't write The No Glam Show to entertain. I wrote it to connect—to start a conversation, to reflect a truth, to honor the ordinary with honesty.

Thank you for picking up this book. I hope you find a part of yourself in these pages.

— Kanika Bhatia Tomar

Acknowledgements

This book would not have been possible without the many voices, hearts, and hands that supported me along the way.

To my family—thank you for the love, the stories, the strength, and the silences. You've shaped more of this book than you know.

To Aelika and Rahul—your belief in me never wavered, even when mine did. Aelika, your constant encouragement was my anchor. Rahul, your quiet strength gave me the space to create. I am endlessly grateful.

To my friends who read early drafts, who listened patiently, who reminded me to keep going—thank you. Your feedback, honesty, and faith meant the world.

To every woman who shared her truth with me, knowingly or unknowingly—you gave voice to Kiara.

And finally, to the readers—thank you for choosing this book. Thank you for your time, your trust, and your willingness to step into this world.

This is not just my story. It is, in many ways, ours.

— Kanika Bhatia Tomar

Prologue

December 1987. Delhi.

The winter sun glowed softly over the city, casting golden light on rooftops and bougainvillea. Inside a bustling household, laughter mingled with the clinking of bangles and the rhythm of dholaks. It was a happy wedding—simple by some standards, but perfect in the eyes of those who mattered.

Two families came together that day not out of obligation, but with warmth, blessings, and the quiet certainty that this match was meant to be. A match made in heaven, they said—and they meant it.

Ten months later, Kiara was born. The first girl child in generations, her arrival filled the home with fresh joy, noisy celebrations, and endless cups of chai for every visitor who came to admire her bright eyes and curious smile.

She grew up surrounded by people—grandparents, uncles, aunts, cousins—all under one roof. A house alive with traditions, stories, and the comforting chaos of joint family life. There was always someone to talk to, someone to argue with, someone to learn from.

But even in the happiest homes, questions bloom quietly. Kiara didn't know it then, but hers would be a journey of looking beneath the surface—of finding herself not in grand gestures, but in the quiet moments that others often overlooked.

This is her story.
Of growing up. Of seeing things as they are.
Of learning that even in the most loving families, not everything is spoken out loud.

CHAPTER ONE

December, 1987

This story begins in the late 1980s—a time when choices were often made by tradition, and marriage was less about romance and more about responsibility, respect, and quiet understanding. She was young, just stepping into womanhood, when it was decided that she would marry him—a man she had known all her life. Not a stranger, not quite a friend, but a familiar face from distant family ties.

There had never been courtship, no grand declarations. Their union was anticipated for years, quietly accepted by both families as something that would one day happen. And in December 1987, beneath the muted glow of wedding lights and the scent of incense and marigold, it did.

She moved into his family's home, a traditional joint household filled with the steady rhythm of daily life—his parents, elder brother, sister-in-law, and their little boy. It was a world of shared meals, folded saris, whispered routines, and generations under one roof.

Nine months later, she brought new life into that home—a baby girl. The first girl born into the family in years. The father was elated, the household lit up with joy. And in that moment, the quiet story of their lives began to unfold in color.

Although she wasn't the only child in the house, Kiara quickly became its heartbeat. Not because she was extraordinary, but because the house had once forgotten what it felt like to have a baby girl within its walls. Her presence was a gentle return—soft, radiant, and unexpected.

She arrived on her grandmother's birthday, a poetic twist of fate that wrapped generations together in one breath. What greater gift could grandparents ask for than the sound of a newborn's cry echoing on the day they celebrated their own life? Perhaps that's why Kiara was held a little closer, spoken to a little softer, and smiled at just a little longer.

In the weeks that followed, she became more than a presence—she became the pulse of the home. Her first word, a tender "Papa," brought tears to eyes and smiles to tired faces. Her first steps came quietly, but not without impact. And before her first birthday arrived, Kiara wasn't just walking—she was running, turning every room into a playground, every hallway into a game of chase.

Her cousin, just two and a half years older, became her first partner-in-crime—part shadow, part sibling, part cheerleader. The house brimmed with their laughter, their tiny disagreements, their shared delight in discovering the world one toy, one cupboard, one puddle at a time.

Even mealtimes became a family mission. The dinner table, once a space for quiet meals, now revolved around a single task: making sure Kiara ate her dinner. One bite from each family member—that was the unspoken rule. One from her mother's hand, one from her aunt, one from her cousin, and of course, a special one from her grandfather, which almost always ended in giggles and a messy spoon.

And then, just like that, the day arrived—Kiara's first birthday.

The house shimmered with anticipation. Fairy lights twinkled across balconies, pastel balloons floated in bunches, and the scent of marigolds and vanilla guitar shaped cake filled the air. It wasn't just a birthday—it was a celebration of love, of life, of everything she had brought into their world.

Guests arrived one after another—family, friends, neighbours—each carrying a gift chosen with thought, each face lighting up as they stepped into the magical scene created for one very special one-year-old. The gifts were perfect in their simplicity: plush toys, picture books, musical rattles, and tiny dresses sewn with care.

It was a gala night, not in extravagance, but in emotion. The kind of night where laughter came easily, music played softly, and every adult momentarily became a child again—awed by Kiara's presence, charmed by her laughter, and overwhelmed by the memories she had created in just twelve short months.

Long after the last song was played and the last guest departed, the house stood a little stiller, the fairy lights still flickering gently in the dark. Kiara was now one. And in that single year, she had not only learned to walk and speak—she had unknowingly taught the family how to feel again. How to pause. How to delight in small joys. How to turn an ordinary day into something worth remembering.

And deep down, everyone knew—
This was just the beginning.

CHAPTER TWO

The Year of Mischiefs

The year and a half after her first birthday slipped by like a soft breeze — full of little milestones, fleeting giggles, and a thousand tiny discoveries. And then, almost without warning, it was time for a new chapter: her very first day of playschool.

Her parents had searched with quiet determination, visiting classrooms and chatting with teachers, until they found the one that felt just right — a place that spoke not just to their hopes, but to her spirit.

That morning, she stood at the door with a high fountain ponytail, wearing a blue dungaree skirt and a crisp white shirt. She looked like a tiny explorer dressed for her first adventure — nervous perhaps, but mostly excited.

But what truly made her feel special was the bag slung over her shoulder. It wasn't sparkly or covered in cartoon characters. Instead, it was printed from top to bottom with colourful alphabets — A to Z dancing across the fabric like a song waiting to be sung. To her, that bag was everything. She carried it not just with pride, but with purpose, as if the printed letters were her passport into this new world.

She didn't know what all the letters meant just yet. But she knew they meant something big. And in that moment, she flaunted the bag like it was the finest thing she'd ever owned.

Most parents had told them — the first day of playschool rarely came without tears. Toddlers, unfamiliar with separation, often clung to their parents, their cries echoing down colourful hallways. Naturally, they braced themselves for the same. But Kiara had something else in mind.

Dressed in her little blue dungarees and alphabet-printed school bag slung proudly over her shoulder, she stood with a calm curiosity in her eyes — not fear. She looked around, noticed the children crying, the tight embraces, the wet cheeks — and for a moment, she hesitated. A tiny wrinkle formed on her brow. This wasn't exactly how she'd imagined it.

But then, like a switch had been flipped, she turned to her parents, flashed a wide, confident smile, and waved — not a shy, uncertain flutter, but a bold, full goodbye. She was ready. Ready to step into her new world, ready to find out what lay behind the school gate.

Inside, where some children whimpered and curled into corners, Kiara danced — quite literally — to her own tunes. She tapped her feet to the rhythm of the morning song, clapped along with the rhymes, and greeted her teachers with a cheerful "hello" that caught them pleasantly off guard. It was as if she had been waiting for this moment far longer than anyone had known.

That day, she sang her first classroom rhyme, mimicked a butterfly with her hands, and laughed at jokes that only children understand. But more than that — she made her very first friends. Tiny faces with uncertain expressions who slowly opened up in response to her warmth, following her lead into the songs, the dances, the games.

It wasn't just the first day of school. It was her first real step into the world — and Kiara took it with joy, courage, and a rhythm all her own.

Kiara had always been a little star in her own right. With her twinkling eyes, dimpled smile, and a voice that bubbled with cheer, she had a way of lighting up any room she walked into. Strangers often stopped mid-step just to smile at her. On walks with her mother, it wasn't uncommon for passersby—completely unknown to them—to lean down and say, "What a happy little girl!"

There was something irresistible about Kiara's joy. She would hum, twirl, laugh at the wind, and above all—she sang. Her latest obsession was a catchy jingle from a television ad that played often in their home. She had memorized it word for word, note for note, and would perform it with such animated flair that her family couldn't help but join in her amusement.

Then came a day that would quietly alter the course of her little world.

A prominent minister happened to visit a neighboring household—an event that created quite a buzz down the lane. The neighbors, eager to impress, invited Kiara's mother and Kiara over, casually mentioning the girl's charm and her famous jingle. Kiara, in her usual free-spirited manner, sang it once more—unbothered by titles or prestige, simply doing what she loved.

To everyone's surprise, the minister laughed heartily, clapped, and turned to Kiara's mother with an unexpected offer. The very product Kiara adored and sang about—they were planning a new advertisement campaign for it. And wouldn't it be perfect, he said, to have a child who already loved it, who brought the song to life without even trying?

It was one of those rare, magical moments when a child's innocent love for a melody met the eyes of someone who could change her world. For Kiara, it wasn't about the cameras or the lights. It was about singing the tune she adored, now on a stage that matched the sparkle she carried every day.

CHAPTER THREE

The No Glam Show

The offer hit the household like a bolt of lightning—brilliant, unexpected, and electrifying. For a moment, time itself seemed to pause. The chatter turned into gasps, eyes widened in disbelief, and Kiara's little cousins ran around the room, not entirely understanding what had happened but feeding off the energy. It was a moment that shimmered with the kind of excitement that made your heart race and your feet restless.

Everyone was talking at once—uncles speculating, aunts whispering, Kiara's father looking stunned into his teacup. But in the center of it all, Kiara's mother sat quietly. Her face carried the kind of stillness that didn't come from shock but from a deeper place—an instinct that understood the weight of what had just occurred.

She had told the minister, with grace and caution, that she would need to speak with her family before giving an answer. Not out of hesitation, but out of respect. Respect for the traditions they followed, for the wisdom of elders who had seen the world change in ways her generation couldn't yet grasp.

That night, long after the house had grown quiet and the excitement had faded into gentle murmurs, she lay in bed staring at the ceiling fan above her. The blades spun endlessly, much like her thoughts. Questions buzzed in her mind. Was this the right step? What would this mean for Kiara? Was she being swept up by a moment, or was this destiny knocking with its soft, persuasive rhythm?

By sunrise, she had made up her mind. She would revisit the past to make sense of the future. She went straight to Kiara's grandparents—keepers of stories, voices of reason. The kettle whistled in the background as they all sat together in the verandah, the early light casting long shadows on the stone floor.

There, amid the comforting scent of ginger tea and old books, the conversation turned earnest. The excitement was now replaced by reflection. Because back in their time—back in the 1980s—television wasn't the glowing centerpiece of every living room. It was rare, a luxury, even a mystery. And for those who encountered it, it wasn't about glamour. It was about windows—windows into knowledge, science, storytelling, and the outside world they had only read about in magazines.

For them, appearing on television wasn't a pursuit of fame. It was a serious calling. A bridge between tradition and progress. An invitation to explore and to educate. The grandparents listened patiently, nodded thoughtfully, and shared their own memories of a simpler, slower era—where choices were deliberate, and values came before visibility.

The house that had been echoing with celebration was now filled with a softer, more introspective silence. Every family member was deep in thought. They understood this was no ordinary opportunity. This was not a show for glam. This was a show of character. Of curiosity. Of change.

And perhaps, it was exactly what Kiara needed.

Just then, the room settled as Kiara's grandfather cleared

his throat. The answer came not in haste, but with utter politeness and quiet conviction—his voice steady, shaped by years of telling stories that mattered.

"No," he said gently, "not now."

A hush followed, not out of disappointment, but out of deep respect. His words held weight—not just because he was the elder, but because he had lived a life rooted in reality. A journalist in his time, he had seen the world beyond the headlines and the cameras. He understood the charm and the chaos that often came hand in hand with public life.

"I understand the opportunity," he continued, his eyes meeting Kiara's mother's with calm assurance. "But if she truly holds the talent—if it's meant for her—this chance will come again. And perhaps at a time when we're ready to hold it with both hands."

For a moment, the family sat in reflective silence. Then slowly, one by one, they began to nod. Not out of obligation, but with the quiet understanding that some decisions, while hard, are right. Kiara's mother let out a breath she hadn't realised she'd been holding. Deep down, she knew it too—they weren't ready, not just yet.

Life resumed its rhythm. The excitement faded, but there was no regret—only a comforting clarity.

A few months later, the very same ad Kiara had once been offered aired on television. The jingle played, the visuals sparkled, and a different child now grinned into the camera. But instead of what-ifs or second guesses, the family smiled.

They laughed at the catchy lines, praised the production, and even hummed along. Kiara, as usual, was dancing to the jingle in her own world—carefree and full of light. Not on the screen, perhaps, but still the star of their little world.

And that, they knew, was more than enough.

CHAPTER FOUR

Gateway to the Formal Schooling

The day had finally arrived—the one every parent both anticipates and dreads. It was time for Kiara to begin her journey into formal schooling. A step that promised bigger goals, structured days, and endless possibilities. Gone would be the carefree hours of play school, where naptime and nursery rhymes ruled the day. Ahead lay uniforms, timetables, interviews, and expectations.

The play school had already begun calling parents in, handing out forms, and quietly slipping in reminders about interview preparations. It wasn't just the children who needed training—it was the parents too. Whispered conversations in the corridors revolved around school reputations, admission timelines, and whispered names of interviewers who could make or break a toddler's academic future.

But Kiara, in the midst of it all, remained gloriously untouched by the frenzy around her. She was still wrapped in the cocoon of her present—dancing freely, snacking endlessly, and weaving stories with her toys. The world was preparing her for the future, but she was still basking in the joy of now.

Then came a day that would become a family classic—one of those moments that, years later, would still trigger laughter at dinner tables.

It started with a regular PTA meeting invite. Kiara's father, who was away on a work trip, couldn't make it. So Kiara's mother requested her brother-in-law—Kiara's jovial, ever-supportive uncle—to accompany her. The next morning, they headed to the school. The waiting area was packed with anxious parents, each one expecting to be gently (or not-so-gently) reprimanded about their child's habits.

Most conversations they overheard were about lunchboxes. Teachers were politely urging parents to reduce portion sizes because the little ones were unable to finish their meals. When it was their turn, Kiara's mother and uncle braced themselves, expecting to hear something along the same lines—perhaps that Kiara was distracted, too chatty, or not eating properly.

But instead, the teacher looked up with a gentle smile and said, "Please send a slightly larger lunch portion for Kiara."

They blinked.

"She tends to eat from other children's tiffins once she's done with hers," the teacher added, trying not to chuckle.

For a moment, there was stunned silence. Then Kiara's mom and uncle exchanged a glance—equal parts mortified and amused—and laughed softly. They nodded, thanked the teacher, and left. It was a quiet ride back home, the streets humming with the usual midday lull. The house, too, was unusually silent. The afternoon sun slanted through the curtains, as most of the family rested or were away at work.

It wasn't until 5 o'clock, when Kiara's grandfather returned from the office, that the house stirred back to life.

Evening tea was a daily ritual, and this one promised a little extra flavor. As he settled into his chair, he asked casually, "So, how was the school meeting?"

That was the cue. Kiara's uncle and mother couldn't hold it in—they burst into laughter, recounting every word of the teacher's comment. The story rolled out, with exaggerated expressions and theatrical pauses, and soon the entire room was laughing. Even Kiara, not understanding a word but sensing the cheer, joined in with her contagious giggles.

Later that evening, when Kiara's father called from out of town, the story was retold with equal enthusiasm. It had officially become a family anecdote—part comedy, part pride, and all heart.

As the laughter faded, life moved on. The last days of play school ticked by, and soon the family returned to the more serious task of selecting the right school. Forms were filled out again, photographs carefully pasted, and documents organized into neat folders. The interviews loomed ahead, bringing with them a new chapter of nervous anticipation.

But through it all, Kiara remained herself—wide-eyed, full of wonder, and always ready for her next snack.

CHAPTER FIVE

The Formal Schooling

Finally, the day had arrived—the day when Kiara was to face her first school interviews. It was time to see how much she had absorbed in play school, how confidently she could respond, and how ready she was to step into a more structured world. Her parents had been diligent, applying to four of the top schools in Delhi, carefully weighing reputation, values, and location. By a stroke of luck—or perhaps fate—they received interview calls from all four.

This was the first.

The school stood tall and proud in the heart of Delhi, with a reputation that spoke of academic excellence and discipline. As they waited outside the interview room, Kiara's parents exchanged anxious glances. The clipboard, the documents, the formal shoes—it all felt very official. Their nervousness was almost tangible. But Kiara? She sat swinging her legs in rhythm, unfazed, as if she were waiting for a birthday party to begin.

Then came the voice from inside the room. "Kiara, please come in."

She stood up instantly, adjusting her little dress with practiced ease. With the air of a princess summoned to her court, she walked in confidently, her parents trailing behind, still holding their breath.

The interviewer greeted them warmly. He asked Kiara for her name, to which she responded with bright eyes and a crystal-clear voice. While the documents were being handed over by her parents, the interviewer began asking Kiara a series of simple questions. Colors, numbers, fruits, animals—she answered each one with enthusiasm and innocence, her confidence growing with every response.

Then came the curveball—the trick questions meant to test her thinking.

The interviewer placed a small toy bus in front of her and asked gently, "Kiara, who drives the bus?"

Kiara looked at the toy bus for a moment, her eyes twinkling. Then, with a broad grin, she said, "Me!"

The interviewer blinked, amused. "Hmm, and who drives a real bus, Kiara?"

Without missing a beat, she looked at him again and repeated proudly, "Me!"

There was a soft chuckle in the room, but the interviewer moved on. He placed a bowl of candies on the table and asked Kiara to pick one for each member of her family. Without hesitation, she began: "One for Papaji... one for Mumma... Badi Mumma... Bade Papa... Bhai... Aditi... Mumma again... Papa..." She named them all—every person in her joint family, with careful selection and an endearing sense of fairness.

Then came the follow-up: "How many siblings do you have?"

Kiara smiled and held up two fingers. "Two," she said with certainty.

The interviewer raised an eyebrow. "You have two siblings?"

"Yes," she nodded. "Bhai and Aditi."

He glanced at the parents. Her mother smiled softly, knowing exactly what had happened.

"And how many moms and dads do you have?" he continued, now curious.

Kiara beamed. "Two papas and two mummas."

That was it. The interview was done.

They left the room, still smiling. They didn't need to be told—deep down, they already knew. Kiara hadn't given the "right" answers. Not the ones rehearsed by countless children being prepped for these very moments. But she had spoken from her heart. With innocence, honesty, and clarity that only a child raised in a house full of love could offer.

Weeks later, the rejection letter came. As expected, she had not been selected. The interviewer, it seemed, had been looking for textbook responses. But Kiara's parents weren't disappointed.

They were, in fact, in awe.

Because in those ten minutes, their daughter had shown them the true meaning of family—not as a structure of labels, but as a lived experience of togetherness. To Kiara, cousins were siblings, and uncles and aunts were as essential as parents. In her world, love was shared, names were interchangeable, and everyone had a candy.

And that was a lesson no school could teach.

CHAPTER SIX

The Final Test

The second and third interviews were unlike the first—for these, only the parents were invited. While that should have made things easier, both experiences left Kiara's parents unsettled.

The second school had the polished exterior and shiny promise of a good institution, but something felt amiss. The environment was rigid, transactional. Despite Kiara clearing the entrance assessment, her parents left with a quiet certainty—they couldn't see their daughter thriving there.

But it was the third school that left a mark—particularly on Kiara's mother. One she would carry with her for the rest of her life.

In the early '90s, not every parent was fluent in English. In fact, it wasn't even a yardstick for intelligence in most Indian homes—it was just another language. But the interviewer at the third school didn't seem to agree. Midway through the session, he looked at Kiara's mother and asked, "Are you comfortable speaking in English?"

She smiled politely and replied with quiet honesty, "I'm not completely hands-on, but I can guide Kiara in her studies."

The interviewer raised his eyebrows. "If you don't understand the language well, how will you teach your child?"

There was a pause. A moment of silence that held more power than any argument.

Then, Kiara's mother looked at him directly and asked, "Does your mother speak English?"

The man looked taken aback. "I... what do you mean?" he said, unsure.

"I mean," she continued, her voice calm but firm, "even if your mother didn't speak English, you're still here, aren't you? Taking interviews. Holding a respectable position. Likewise, Kiara can do the same. A mother's strength isn't in her language—it's in her intent."

There was no further discussion needed. Kiara's parents knew—this wasn't the place for their daughter. The interviewer, perhaps trying to regain control of the conversation, mentioned that Kiara had cleared the second school interview. "Why don't you admit her there?" he suggested.

"We didn't like the management," Kiara's father replied curtly.

The interviewer smirked, "But both schools have almost the same management."

"Then that only confirms we're not interested at all," her father replied without hesitation. "Especially after the way you spoke to my wife."

They got up and left without so much as a thank you.

Now, only one school remained. The final interview. And something about it felt right from the start.

Two days later, Kiara was dressed in a bright red dress, speckled with colorful flowers—little bursts of pink, blue, yellow, and green dancing across the fabric. She looked like a splash of joy in motion.

As they entered the school gate, she saw swings, a spacious ground, and smiling teachers greeting children as they passed. There was warmth in the air, a sense of welcome that felt genuine.

Inside, the interview room looked more like a playroom than a boardroom—colorful chairs, cheerful toys, and storybooks lined the shelves. The interviewer greeted them with a smile that reached his eyes, and Kiara, in her usual confident way, stepped forward, completely at ease.

As the initial questions were directed at the parents, Kiara wandered toward a pile of picture books before being gently invited to take her seat.

"Kiara," the teacher asked with a kind smile, "what color is your dress?"

"Red!" she said brightly.

The interviewer leaned in playfully. "Hmm... but it looks pink to me."

Kiara paused, glanced down at her dress, then smiled. "You could be right," she said thoughtfully. "It has pink, blue, yellow, and green flowers. But the main color is red."

There was a brief silence—then laughter. Not the polite kind, but the delighted kind. The interviewer was visibly impressed, not just by her intelligence but by her composure and clarity.

They moved on to basic math, objects, colors, and a few situational questions. Kiara responded with the same charm and childlike clarity that had made her family fall in love with her answers over and over again.

When they walked out, there was no need to say anything. Everyone felt it. This time—it was right.

Four days later, the list was pinned on the school's notice board. Kiara's name was there, written in crisp black letters. Her parents stared at it for a long moment, letting the quiet pride sink in.

This was it.

Kiara had found her school—the one that would shape her beginnings, challenge her mind, and nurture her spirit.

The chapter of playtime innocence had closed, and the world of learning had begun.

And as she skipped down the corridor that day, still twirling in her red dress, everyone knew—this was just the start.

CHAPTER SEVEN

First Day at Formal School

The sun rose a little brighter that day, as if it, too, was aware that something special was about to begin.

Kiara stood in front of the mirror, dressed in her crisp new school uniform—a navy pinafore, white shirt, white socks folded just right, and a neat pair of black shoes that still squeaked when she walked. Her mother had parted her hair carefully and tied it into two perfect ponytails, each fastened with red ribbons that matched the little apple on her name badge. She looked like a dream, glowing with excitement and pride.

To her family, she wasn't just heading to school. She was stepping into a new chapter—one that came with bells, books, timetables, and a world far beyond nursery rhymes and nap time. Her grandparents watched from the doorway, her father clicked a dozen photos, and her mother, though smiling, couldn't stop smoothing down invisible creases on her uniform.

Kiara, unaware of the quiet emotion swirling around her, twirled once and declared, "I'm ready!"

As they arrived at the school gates, Kiara's eyes scanned the grand building—the school of her dreams. It had tall gates, smiling guards, and a sea of children in matching uniforms. A few cried, some clung to their parents, and others marched ahead confidently. Kiara stood in the middle—curious, excited, but with just a flicker of hesitation in her eyes.

And then she heard it. A burst of laughter.

"Kiara!"

She turned.

There they were—her friends from play school, waving frantically, their backpacks bouncing as they ran up to her. Her face lit up like a firecracker. In that instant, every trace of nervousness disappeared. She waved back, ran toward them, and hugged them like they hadn't met in years.

Inside the classroom, Montessori One, the scene was something out of a storybook. The walls were painted in soft pastels with clouds, rainbows, and tiny cartoon pencils. Everything was built for little hands—low benches, open shelves, baskets full of books and toys, and tiny chairs arranged in a colorful semicircle.

Kiara and her friends settled in like they'd always belonged. The teacher walked in, a kind-faced woman in a soft cotton sari with a voice that felt like a lullaby. She introduced herself and welcomed each child by name, making every little one feel important.

Then came the introductions.

Some kids stood awkwardly, mumbling their names. Others sang them proudly. When it was Kiara's turn, she stood up, smiled, and said her name like she was performing on stage. "My name is Kiara! I love to dance, I like red, and I can eat a whole bowl of mangoes!" The class giggled, the teacher chuckled, and Kiara sat down, proud of her very first performance.

The rest of the day passed in a blur of discovery. There were counting games with colorful beads, a story circle where they learned about a cat who wore shoes, and a mini tour of the school playground. Kiara spotted swings and monkey bars and made a mental note to claim the highest one during recess.

At snack time, the children sat on floor mats, unzipping tiffins and trading bits of food like secret treasures. Kiara, true to tradition, shared her paratha roll and ended up with a chocolate biscuit and a tiny packet of mango juice in return.

By the end of the day, she had not just attended school—she had owned it.

Meanwhile, at home, the hours ticked by slowly. Her grandparents kept glancing at the clock. Her mother, pretending to be busy in the kitchen, peeked out the window every few minutes. Her father, stuck in office, kept calling, "She must be back by now, right? What did she say?"

When the door finally opened, in came Kiara—hair slightly messy, socks rolled down, and shoes covered in playground dust. But her smile? That hadn't faded one bit.

The house sprang to life.

Her grandparents gathered around. Her mother sat beside her with juice. And Kiara began—animated, dramatic, her arms flailing as she narrated every detail. From the classroom toys to the color of her friend's lunchbox, she spared nothing. She paused only to breathe.

That evening, when her father returned from work, she retold everything again—this time with added flourishes and exaggerated expressions. He laughed, pulled her into a hug, and told her he was proud.

Later that night, after dinner, she curled up beside her mother with her toy bunny, sleeping slowly tugging at her eyelids. "I think I'll go again tomorrow," she whispered.

Her mother smiled and kissed her forehead. "You'll go every day now."

Kiara grinned, already drifting into dreams. "Then I'll make new stories every day."

And just like that, the first page of her school life was written—filled with laughter, red ribbons, friends, and the beginning of a thousand little adventures.

CHAPTER EIGHT

The Separation

It was the early '90s, a time when Indian cities were expanding, and the concept of apartment living—societies, as they came to be known—was still catching on. Kiara's joint family had long lived under one roof, a home that echoed with laughter, shared meals, and the chaos only a house full of children and multigenerational love can create.

But even love sometimes needs more room to breathe.

As the children grew and the family expanded, the house began to feel smaller. It wasn't just about space—it was about privacy, personal routines, and the quiet, practical needs of a growing family. The conversations started as gentle murmurs over evening tea but gradually turned into real discussions. Everyone knew change was coming. And eventually, it did.

One day, the children were gently gathered and told: they would soon be moving. It wasn't a goodbye—it was a shift. Kiara's father and uncle had decided to move into a newly developing housing society nearby. The original plan had been ideal—both brothers in the same society, a few buildings apart, continuing the same rhythm in a new setting.

But fate, in the form of a housing draw, had other plans.

Society allotments in those days weren't simply booked—they were won. After paying the booking amount, names were drawn, and apartments were assigned. Kiara's uncle turned out to be lucky. He secured a flat in the newly built tower. But Kiara's family didn't get the same result. Their name wasn't picked.

After much thought, it was decided that Kiara's parents would take a rented apartment in the neighboring society. Close enough to visit every day. Close enough to keep the bond alive.

The bigger question was about the grandparents.

Kiara's uncle and aunt were both working professionals with demanding jobs. Kiara's mother, however, was a homemaker. Though she'd recently completed a beautician's course while Kiara was at school, her schedule was still more flexible. It was decided, practically and lovingly, that the grandparents would stay with Kiara's uncle to help care for the children—but every evening, they would walk over to Kiara's house, keeping the thread of togetherness unbroken.

And so, the shifting began.

Boxes were packed, rooms were cleared, and familiar walls were left behind. The first few nights in the new home were quieter. Different. Kiara missed the clatter of overlapping routines, the smell of her aunt's morning coffee mixing with her mother's tadka, and the chorus of good-nights shared across rooms.

But children adapt faster than adults.

Within a week, Kiara had found her new corner to sit in with her books, her new window to look out from, and a new set of stairs to run down when the school bus arrived. The rented flat began to feel like home.

Her mother quickly settled into a rhythm too.

Each morning, she would rise before dawn, preparing lunchboxes for both Kiara and her father. Once they had left—Kiara with her bright pink backpack and her father with his briefcase—she would clear the breakfast table and then head into her small, sunlit corner, where she practiced what she had learned during her beauty course. Sometimes she worked on her own hair, sometimes she experimented with mehndi designs, sometimes she practiced threading on cotton rolls. It was her little ambition, her quiet dream growing alongside her daughter.

By noon, she'd be at the bus stand, waiting for Kiara with a gentle smile and a bottle of chilled water. Kiara, tired and chatty, would narrate her day as they walked home, hand in hand. They would eat together, their laughter echoing in the walls that had once felt too silent. Then came the homework hour—books opened, pencils chewed, and her mother's gentle coaxing turning into playful bribes.

And like clockwork, by 5 PM, the front doorbell would ring.

The grandparents had arrived.

Every single day.

It didn't matter how hot it was or how tired they felt. That ritual walk from one society to another became their sacred thread, connecting what had been separated by logistics but not by love. And when they arrived, the house would come alive again. Kiara would break into mischief mode, showing off her drawings, enacting school stories, and climbing all over her grandfather as if nothing had changed.

The evenings were full of warmth—stories, laughter, and sometimes mild scoldings when Kiara got too wild. Dinner was served family-style, on the floor or around the small dining table, just like old times. After the last bite and a final round of jokes, the grandparents would gather their shawls and slippers and walk back to the other house—until the next evening.

Over time, this routine settled into something comforting, almost sacred. The physical walls had changed, but the emotional bridges remained intact.

What began as a separation became a new way of being together.

CHAPTER NINE

The Good News

While the families now lived apart, the love between them stayed untouched. Whether it was Rakhi, Diwali, or Holi, every festival was still celebrated under one roof at Kiara's uncle and aunt's home—just like old times.

Kiara, now growing a little older, had started to feel the change. Back in the early '90s, life wasn't filled with gadgets and cartoons like today. The only sources of entertainment were TV, radio, and playing outside. Cable television was still new, and most of the content wasn't kid-friendly. Kiara missed having someone to share her games and stories with—especially her cousins.

That's when she started asking for a sibling.

And not just asking—demanding. Day and night.

She didn't understand that babies couldn't just be picked off a supermarket shelf. For her, it was a simple request. "I want my own brother," she'd say, in front of anyone—guests, neighbors, even during temple visits. Her mother would go red with embarrassment, but Kiara was unstoppable.

At the temple, she would stand in front of Lord Krishna's idol and say loudly, "Please give me a brother like you. I'll name him Kunal." Her mother would try to hush her, but it was too late. The prayer was out in the open, and anyone within earshot had heard.

Eventually, the parents began to seriously think about the little one's wish. And soon, the big news arrived—Kiara's mother was expecting.

A wave of joy spread through the family. Kiara's grandparents began spending more time at her house, helping her mom through the pregnancy and managing daily life. Her grandmother, especially, would balance household chores and still find time to play board games with Kiara or tell her stories while oiling her hair.

Days turned to weeks, weeks into months.

Then one night, it happened.

Kiara's mom felt discomfort and had to be rushed to the hospital. It was a stormy evening. The sky was pitch black, the wind howled through the streets, and the moment they reached the hospital, rain started pouring heavily. So heavily, in fact, that water began seeping into the hospital elevators, and the nearby power supply started to flicker and fail.

It was chaos.

And in the middle of it all, Kiara's mom made a sudden, very unexpected demand.

A pure vegetarian all her life, she looked at the female doctor and said, "I want to eat chicken."

The doctor paused, surprised. "Chicken?" she asked, unsure if she had heard correctly.

"Yes," Kiara's mom nodded. "Just a little. I don't know why—but I really want it now."

Amused and slightly confused, the doctor managed to arrange for a pill-sized piece, just to satisfy her craving. She ate it calmly, and not long after, she went into labor.

And then, at just one hour past midnight, in the middle of the storm and power outages, Kiara's wish came true.

Her baby brother was born.

The next morning, the hospital room filled with giggles and excitement. Kiara and her cousins arrived to see the new family member—still dressed in their school uniforms, ready to go straight to class after the visit. But nothing could stop Kiara's excitement.

She rushed to see the baby and insisted on holding him. But her little hands couldn't manage, and the nurse had to help her simply touch his fingers. Still, that was enough. Her face lit up with pride.

"I'm a big sister now," she announced to everyone.

She was six years older than her baby brother—and already completely in love.

That day, she refused to go to school.

And for once, no one objected.

She stayed by her mother's side, whispering stories to the sleeping newborn, and smiling so wide, it was hard to believe she had ever been lonely.

Her brother had arrived.

Her world was complete.

Two's Company

The house felt different now.

Livelier. Louder. And definitely messier.

With the arrival of Kiara's baby brother—Kunal, as she had lovingly named him even before he was born—everything changed. But not in a disruptive way. It was as though a missing piece had finally clicked into place. The once-quiet corners now echoed with coos and cries, the tidy living room had been invaded by rattles and feeding bottles, and Kiara... Kiara had stepped into a brand-new role.

The Big Sister.

It wasn't just a title. It was her new identity, and she wore it with pride.

From the moment Kunal came home, Kiara appointed herself as his unofficial assistant. She was there for everything—from handing diapers to guarding his cradle like a soldier on duty. She'd lean over the crib every morning, whispering, "Good morning, Kunal. Did you miss me?" and when he smiled in his sleep, she'd run to announce to everyone, "He smiled because of me!"

Her parents watched her with a mix of amusement and admiration. There was a new spark in her—an eagerness, a sense of responsibility that made her seem older overnight.

She was still mischievous, of course, still danced around the house, but now there was someone she was dancing for.

Kunal.

The two of them were six years apart, but Kiara didn't see it that way. For her, they were a team. Two explorers in a world of grown-ups. Two partners in stories only they understood. She'd sit beside him, show him her school books, try to teach him the alphabet, and once even attempted to feed him a bit of her biscuit when no one was looking.

"Don't do that," her mother had warned gently. "He's not ready."

"But he looked like he wanted one!" Kiara had argued, genuinely confused why someone so tiny couldn't share a snack.

As the months passed, the bond deepened.

Kiara would come home from school, fling her bag aside, and rush to the cradle before even taking her shoes off. Sometimes she'd be rewarded with a gummy grin, other times with a loud cry—but it didn't matter. She was his person. And he was hers.

The routine of the house had adjusted to accommodate both.

Mornings were now about double the hustle—getting Kiara ready for school while managing Kunal's unpredictable sleep schedule. But her mother handled it with practiced ease. She would make breakfast, prepare lunchboxes, rock Kunal to sleep, and still manage to slip in time to listen to Kiara's school stories.

Evenings became their golden hours. After homework and a snack, Kiara would lie on the floor next to Kunal's playmat, making faces, singing songs, or telling him made-up tales about magical birds and flying bicycles. He'd wave his tiny fists, gurgle, and kick in excitement. Their laughter blended into the walls.

Their favorite time, however, was at night.

After dinner, Kiara would insist on one last moment with her baby brother before bedtime. "Just one goodnight kiss," she'd say, and tiptoe into his room. She'd place a soft kiss on his forehead and whisper, "Sleep tight, my Kunal. I'm here."

Her parents would watch quietly from the doorway, holding each other's hand, their hearts full.

Two's company, they thought.

And what a beautiful company it was.

CHAPTER ELEVEN

Kunal Started Speaking

It was one of the most heartwarming moments in the family when Kunal, the little bundle of joy, began to speak. For Kiara, it was nothing short of magic. She had waited patiently—or not so patiently—for this day. And when it came, it was every bit as wonderful as she had imagined.

His words were not perfect, often laced with a cute little lisp, but that only made them more endearing. What melted Kiara's heart the most was how he called her—"Tiara." "Kiara" was a bit of a tongue-twister for a toddler, but "Tiara" came out just right... and somehow, it suited her perfectly. She beamed every time he said it, like he'd just crowned her with affection.

Kiara, who once hated sharing—her food, her toys, even her space—now didn't think twice before giving Kunal everything. Whether it was her favorite chocolate or a spot beside her on the couch, he was always first.

Shopping trips with her mom were no longer about her next dress or a sparkly hairband. The moment they entered a store, she would march straight to the boys' section, scan the racks, and pick clothes for her brother. "This one's perfect for Kunal," she'd say, holding up a t-shirt with superheroes or cartoon animals, eyes shining with excitement.

She had changed completely. And beautifully.

But of course, even the sweetest siblings have their moments.

They would fight, as all kids do—with full energy and dramatic flair. From who got the last bite of chocolate to who got to hold the remote control, every day came with its tiny battle. Kunal, though younger, had mastered the art of loud protest, while Kiara had developed the dramatic storm-off. Their mother and grandparents often played peacemaker, only to find them giggling together five minutes later as if nothing ever happened.

And then came that afternoon.

Kiara, in one of her mischievous moods, decided to play hide and seek. But instead of hiding herself, she came up with a "better" idea. She gently picked up Kunal and snuck him under her study table, inside the cabinet that had just enough space for him to sit curled up. She shut the door softly and told him, "Stay here quietly, okay? It's a secret."

Then she ran out and joined the family in the living room, pretending to look surprised. "Mumma, where's Kunal? I can't find him!"

Panic hit like a wave.

The entire house turned into a search zone. Her grandmother started checking every room. Her mother called out from the balcony. Even the watchman downstairs was alerted.

Just as her mother's voice cracked with worry and her grandfather picked up the landline to inform the neighbors, Kiara ran into her room, opened the cabinet, and proudly announced, "Found him!"

Everyone turned, speechless. Kunal blinked in the sudden light, looking quite pleased with himself for having played along so well.

The room fell silent. Then... laughter.

Mixed with relief, a little scolding, and a lot of head-shaking.

"That girl will drive us mad one day," her grandfather mumbled with a chuckle, shaking his head, while her mother sighed in half-anger, half-amusement. "You're lucky you're cute, Kiara."

Then, as time passed, it was Kunal's turn to start formal schooling.

But unlike Kiara's long, anxious school search, this time the journey was smoother. In India, once a child is admitted to a good school, their siblings are usually given priority admission. No endless forms, no scouting dozens of schools—just a date, a slot, and an interview.

And on the day of his interview, the whole family felt a familiar mix of nerves and excitement.

As they entered the school's interview room, a pleasant surprise greeted them—the teacher sitting across the table was none other than Kiara's former class teacher.

A warm smile spread across her face. "Oh! Kiara's little brother?"

Kiara's parents immediately felt a wave of comfort. This was someone who knew their daughter, someone who already understood their family.

The interview began casually, more like a friendly chat than a formal assessment. The teacher turned to Kunal, leaned in with a smile, and said, "Can you recite a poem for me? One in English, and one in Hindi?"

Kunal, ever so slightly shy, nodded. And then, in his signature lisp, he began to sing.

Words spilled out in his tiny, sweet voice—mispronounced, but delivered with the full confidence of a star. The teacher couldn't help but laugh.

"That was too cute to handle," she said. "You don't need to say anything else. Please go ahead and pay the admission fee. Kunal is in."

Before they could thank her, she leaned down and asked Kunal, "Do you want to come to your sister's school?"

Without hesitation, he jumped up, clapped, and shouted, "Yes!"

And just like that, another new chapter began—two siblings, one school, and a thousand adventures waiting just around the corner.

CHAPTER TWELVE

School Days Together

School had officially started for both of us.

But there was a slight time gap—Kunal's school hours began two hours after mine. At first, this turned out to be a small blessing for our mother. Every morning, she would rise early, prepping my lunchbox, combing my hair into neat ponytails, and making breakfast for both me and Dad. Even though Dad left later than me, she preferred to get everything done in one go—no point in repeating the effort.

But now, with Kunal starting school too, she could breathe a little easier. Since he left later, she had the brilliant idea of sending my lunchbox with him. That way, it stayed fresh and warm, and she didn't have to rush through the morning chaos.

And so began a little ritual.

Every day, Kunal would arrive at school with my lunchbox tucked neatly in his backpack. When lunchtime neared, I'd pop over to his class to collect it. The moment he saw me through the classroom door, his little face would light up. He would jump, shout my name (or rather, "Tiara!" in his signature lisp), and rushed over with the tiffin like it was the most important delivery in the world.

At first, it was sweet—even adorable.

But eventually, his excitement started making me late for my next class. I'd end up chatting with him, calming him down, and walking him back to his seat while his classmates watched like it was a scene from a cartoon show. So one day, I gently asked Mom to change the routine. "Can you please stop sending my lunch with Kunal? It's making me late."

She smiled, nodded, and agreed.

But little did I know that this routine would come back—just once—with an unforgettable twist.

It was just before our summer holidays. We were having a class party, and our school didn't believe in ordering outside food. Instead, we had potluck-style celebrations, where every child brought something homemade to share.

I told Mom, "Please pack cutlets and burgers for me."

She did—perfectly wrapped, still warm, and filled with love. But instead of giving the box to me directly, she handed it over to Kunal. "Take this to your sister's class," she said.

And he did—calmly, without fuss.

He walked to my classroom, saw me sitting there, came over, handed me the tiffin, and left. No jumping, no shouting, no drama. It felt strange. Quiet.

But it was the silence before the storm.

You see, junior school hours ended earlier than ours. So Kunal reached home a full hour before I did. And the moment he got home, he launched into a full-blown report—a story so dramatic it could put a Bollywood film to shame.

So when I walked into the house that afternoon, sweaty and tired but happy from the party, I found Mom waiting for me at the door—arms folded, eyes wide, trying to keep a straight face.

"Kunal told me everything," she said.

Now, here's the context. I was in Class 3 at the time, and our seating arrangements rotated weekly. There were no fixed benches, and we didn't get to choose our partners—the teacher decided who sat with whom. That week, I had been paired with a boy and was sitting near the back of the class. Totally normal for us, but for Kunal? Earth-shattering.

Having only ever seen me playing with girls at home, this was clearly a shocking revelation.

In his sweet, broken words, he told Mom that when he walked into my class, he saw me "talking to boys and sitting with them." His tone? Grave. Like he had just uncovered a national secret. And for his age, it was genuinely touching—his concern, his protectiveness, his very serious attempt at being a responsible younger brother.

Mom, to her credit, pretended to take it seriously. "Hmm... really? Boys, you say?"

She played along beautifully, calling in the grandparents and Dad to hear Kunal's breaking news. And of course, he repeated the whole story, eyes wide, arms flailing, like a reporter delivering breaking headlines.

They all nodded solemnly, trying to suppress laughter.

Then came my "scolding." One by one, each family member playfully chided me, just enough to make Kunal feel like his complaint had been heard and respected.

In truth, everyone knew how schools worked—seating rotations, mixed classrooms, shared benches. But they played their parts for his sake. Because for Kunal, it wasn't just a story. It was his first act of looking out for his sister.

And for me?

It was one of the funniest and sweetest days I would never forget.

CHAPTER THIRTEEN

The Summer of Stories

Summer had arrived, wrapping the days in warmth, mangoes, and mischief. The school year was over, and time suddenly felt slower, softer—stretching like melted ice cream on a plate.

Our house shifted into vacation mode. Mornings were lazy, afternoons sweaty, and evenings filled with chatter. And although Dadu and Dadi now lived separately with Kunal and my uncle, they visited us every evening, like clockwork. Dad was only home on Sundays, still busy with office six days a week, gone early and back just in time for dinner.

So most of our long summer days were spent with Mom, Kunal, and me—inventing games, daydreaming, and, as it happened that year, diving deep into stories.

It all began with a power cut.

One boring afternoon, the power went out, the TV went blank, and the house fell into that sleepy silence only a hot day can bring. With nothing else to do, I declared, "Let's tell stories."

Kunal clapped in agreement. And I—armed with imagination and mischief—decided to begin a series of haunted stories.

Ghosts with glowing eyes. Talking mirrors. Footsteps in empty rooms. Shoes that walked by themselves. I made it all up. Dramatically. Pausing in just the right places to whisper "boo" and make Kunal squeal.

At first, he loved it. But soon... it was too much.

He wouldn't go to the bathroom alone. He insisted on keeping the lights on during the day. He even followed me to the kitchen to check if the sugar tin had moved by itself.

One night, he whispered to Mom, "What if Tiara's cupboard has a ghost?"

That was my cue to stop.

So, I did what any guilty storyteller would do—I invented Babli, the good ghost. She only scared bad ghosts, protected brave kids, and lived in our water bottle. Kunal adored her. He started drawing her. Talking about her to Dadi and Dadu. Even told the neighbor aunty she didn't need mosquito repellent because Babli was on duty.

Our haunted summer had transformed into one filled with comic strips, pretend ghost-hunting missions, and laughter echoing in the dark.

But it wasn't just haunted stories that made that summer memorable.

Every now and then, Dad would take us to his office—a real treat back then.

Unlike offices now, his was a true pen-and-paper world, with files stacked high, stamping machines, registers, and calculators that clicked as they punched out numbers. It was a bank, and to us, it was like stepping into a movie.

People came in and out, counting cash, talking softly, and standing in long queues. When we entered, Dad's colleagues would gather around to greet us like we were special guests. The office peon, kind and cheerful, always brought us glasses of Rooh Afza or lemon soda, along with a tray of snacks—biscuits, samosas, or sometimes jalebis.

But the best part came at lunch hour.

Out came a big, shiny carrom board, and the men gathered like champions in a stadium. Dad, of course, was the undisputed carrom king. His strikes were clean, fast, and almost impossible to beat. Watching him play with such confidence made us beam with pride.

Naturally, we wanted one too.

That very week, we convinced Mom to get us a carrom board. And thus began a new ritual—afternoon carrom battles with Mom, and weekend tournaments with Dad.

Mom was decent at it—strategic but not deadly. But Dad? He was a force.

Every match would begin peacefully and end with one of us yelling, "No fair! I wanted to be on Papa's team!"

It became a tradition: me vs. Kunal to win Dad's side. Because whoever teamed up with Dad almost always won.

Mom would laugh and roll her eyes. "One day, you both will have to win on your own," she'd say.

But we weren't listening.

Back then, winning with Dad was all that mattered.

That summer was made of many things—ghost stories, invisible friends, mango juice, slow afternoons, and the soft clack of carrom coins bouncing off wooden corners.

But more than anything, it was made of moments we didn't realize were memories.

Memories that would stay with us long after the power returned... and long after the carrom board gathered dust in the corncr.

CHAPTER FOURTEEN

The Year of Ups and Downs

Some years arrive quietly.

Others enter like a whirlwind—loud, emotional, unpredictable.

This was that kind of year.

For a long time, there had been a dream—to live in the same society as Kiara's uncle, to recreate the warmth of a joint family in two separate flats under the same sky. A flat had been promised. Papers signed. Deposits made. But years went by, and nothing moved. The society kept delaying the allotment. Promises turned into excuses, and hope started to wear thin.

Until one day, Kiara's father had enough.

He packed up a few essentials, furniture, and mattresses from their rented flat and decided to move—unofficially—into one of the still-empty flats in the society where Kiara's uncle lived. It wasn't the allotted one, but it was vacant. His logic was simple: "If they're not giving us what's ours, we'll take what's available."

The family—Kiara, Kunal, and their parents—loaded themselves onto a small truck with their belongings and drove straight to the society. The flat on the ground floor looked untouched. Kiara's father pushed open the door and started unloading.

Tension was thick in the air.

The kids, sensing something big was about to happen, ran straight to their uncle's house. Kiara breathlessly told them everything. Within minutes, her uncle and grandfather rushed to the scene to intervene. They tried to reason with her father, calm him down, explain the consequences. But when someone is hurt by delay, dignity, and disappointment, logic often takes a back seat.

That entire evening felt like a tug-of-war—between frustration and patience, family and legality.

The night passed in unrest.

By morning, tempers had cooled—slightly. The society management stepped in, promised to resolve matters, and eventually returned the deposit that had been lying with them for years.

The furniture was loaded back onto the truck, and the family returned to their rented apartment.

It could have ended there.

A year defined by frustration.

But the universe had other plans.

Later that week, Kiara's father quietly took the family for a drive back into their rented society, only this time to a different lane. As they stood before a new building, he asked them to follow him. He led them to a flat on the first floor, then gently nudged Kiara's mother toward the kitchen window.

"How does this look?" he asked, almost casually.

She peeked inside—a wide kitchen, airy and sunlit, with enough space for dreams to grow.

She smiled. "It's nice."

The next morning, Kiara's father made the announcement.

"This will be our new home."

Just like that, the family's energy shifted from stress to excitement.

They visited the flat again—this time, properly. The rooms were raw, the walls plain, and cement dust still clung to the corners. But the layout felt right. The energy felt warm. The house wasn't perfect yet, but it felt like theirs.

He made the booking payment, and within days, renovation plans began. It wasn't a full overhaul—just a few adjustments here and there. Enough to make it home.

And then came Diwali.

Though the house was still under renovation, Kiara and her mom carried a small box of diyas and went to the site. The workers had gone home early for the festival. The floor was dusty, wires were exposed, and walls half-painted. But the heart? The heart was full.

In that half-constructed space, they lit the first diya.

One after another, small flames flickered to life—a silent blessing for a home that hadn't even begun, but already belonged to them.

Kiara stood near the entrance, holding a diya in her hand, watching her mom light one in the kitchen. The shadows danced on the cemented walls, and a cool breeze rushed through the balcony grills.

It was quiet.

But in that quiet, there was hope.

And sometimes, hope is all a new beginning needs.

That Diwali evening, as Kiara and her mother lit those first diyas in the raw, unfinished flat, none of them knew how much that light would mean in the darkness to come.

A few months later, life seemed to fall into rhythm again.

The new flat's renovations were nearing completion, and the family was beginning to dream of moving in. Amid the planning, Kiara's mother decided to take a small evening off—just a few hours with her husband to shop for curtains, a new mixer, maybe even a dining table.

The plan was simple: the kids would stay back with Dadi—their grandmother—who was already home looking after their uncle's children. It wasn't unusual. Dadi was strong, dependable, and always ready to juggle a house full of grandkids like it was the most natural thing in the world.

Kiara's mother told her, "We'll be back soon, okay? Be good. Help Dadi if she needs anything."

But destiny had something else in mind.

Just five minutes after they left, while they were still at the society gate, they heard footsteps running behind them. It was Kiara and Kunal, breathless, panic in their eyes.

"Dadi fell! Come quick!"

They rushed back to the house—and what they saw would never leave their memory.

Dadi was unconscious, lying on the kitchen floor.

There had been no sound, no call for help. Just silence. Kiara's mother with the help of neighbours lifted her gently and placed her on the bed. They tried everything—massaging her hands, rubbing her feet, calling out to her—but nothing worked.

Within minutes, a cab was called, and she was rushed to thc hospital.

The doctors moved quickly, but the news that followed was crushing: she had slipped into a coma, and was later put on a ventilator.

For two to three days, the family lived in the waiting area, surrounded by machines, prayers, and hope that refused to give up. But eventually, the machines slowed. The monitors flattened.

And just like that... Dadi was gone.

A wave of stillness passed over the entire family. Kiara's grandfather was devastated.

They hadn't just been husband and wife.

They were friends, companions, each other's sounding boards. They finished each other's sentences, laughed at the same silly jokes, and knew the rhythm of each other's thoughts without saying a word.

Losing her was like losing a limb—something essential, something irreplaceable.

In the weeks that followed, he tried to hold himself together—for the kids, for the family. But grief doesn't follow a script. It came to him in quiet moments, in the smell of her clothes, in the sight of her empty chair, in the early mornings when her tea wasn't waiting for him anymore.

Some days, he would lose focus while riding his scooter—once banging it into a footpath, another time losing balance completely and falling off. There were bruises, scratches, and more than anything, a quiet unraveling.

The family began to worry. Kiara, still too young to understand grief in its full shape, watched silently as her grandfather aged in weeks.

But slowly, and with immense courage, he found his center again.

"I have to live for all of you," he once told Kiara's father. "Your mother wouldn't have forgiven me if I gave up now."

He began rebuilding his life—not by forgetting her, but by honoring her memory through every little thing: continuing the evening walks she once loved, telling the grandkids her stories, and making sure every corner of the new home had her presence in spirit.

And so, the year that began with dreams and shifting furniture, ended with candles lit in memory.

A year where the walls of a new home rose, but so did the weight of loss.

A year that taught them that life is not just made of beginnings, but of learning to live through endings too.

And in the quiet strength of a grandfather who stayed—for his children, for his grandchildren—that year of ups and downs found its heartbeat again.

CHAPTER FIFTEEN

The Time Flies

Time, as always, had a way of slipping by without notice.

Kunal was now in primary school, full of questions, boundless energy, and a growing confidence of his own. Kiara, on the other hand, was stepping into a space even she couldn't quite describe. She still loved raisins—her favorite snack of all time—and one afternoon, she quietly finished half the container that her mother had neatly stored in the kitchen.

The next morning, school was off, and Kiara—relieved at the chance to sleep in—woke up later than usual. But she wasn't feeling like herself. There was a strange ache in her lower stomach, one she had never felt before. It wasn't sharp, but persistent—dull, nagging, and unfamiliar. She didn't know what to make of it.

She went about her day anyway—attending her tuition class, laughing with friends, even playing in the evening. But underneath the surface, something didn't feel right. Her stomach ached. And then there was something else. Her undergarments were stained, something she had never experienced before.

She didn't say a word.

Not to her mom. Not to anyone. In her young mind, she wondered if something was wrong. Had she eaten too many raisins? Was she sick? Was this something to hide?

That evening, she went to bed early—her body quietly overwhelmed, her mind confused, and her heart unsure of what to feel.

But mothers always know.

Late that night, her mom came in to check on her, as she always did before sleeping. As she leaned in to tuck Kiara's blanket, her eyes fell on the white floral skirt Kiara had worn to bed.

There it was—a reddish-brown stain, faint but clear.

She gently woke Kiara and sat her up. There was no anger, no panic—just calm care. She helped her change, explained gently what was happening, and showed her how to use a sanitary pad for the first time.

And then, in a quiet ritual passed down from her own childhood, she handed Kiara a pencil and said, "Come with me."

Together, they went to the wall near Kiara's room where little marks from past years still faintly lived. Kiara's mom made Kiara draw three straight lines, then crossed them diagonally with a fourth. Kiara looked at her, puzzled.

"This," her mother said softly, "means it will last for four days. And it will come every month. But don't worry. It's normal. It means you're growing up."

Later that evening, she called Kiara's maternal and paternal aunts, and told them the news. They decided that her maasi (maternal aunt) would visit the following weekend, bringing along Reema, her older daughter who was eight years senior to Kiara. The idea was simple—let someone closer to Kiara's age explain it to her, comfort her, and make her feel less alone.

That week, Kiara was... off. Not exactly sad, not scared either, but unsure. She couldn't process what was happening inside her body. Everything felt foreign. Her stomach still hurt, and the bleeding hadn't stopped. She didn't feel sick, but she didn't feel normal either.

Then the weekend came.

With it arrived her Maasi's family, and along came Reema and Varun—her cousin,Varun was born just forty days apart, and her best buddy in the world. The moment they stepped inside the house, Kiara's gloomy thoughts scattered like birds. The house filled with chatter, laughter, and that rare, comforting noise only cousins bring with them.

Kiara and Varun dove straight into games, jokes, and stories. Reema, meanwhile, helped in the kitchen with Maasi. And though the visit had been planned with the intention of a "woman-to-woman" conversation, Kiara learned absolutely nothing that weekend. She was too busy having fun to remember she was even supposed to learn anything.

By the time they left the next evening, she had laughed more than she had all week.

But the period didn't stop.

It had now been over ten days, and her mother, concerned, decided it was time to visit the family doctor. Kiara sat quietly in the clinic, her hands cold, her thoughts tangled. She wasn't ready for another "new experience."

The doctor smiled kindly, asked a few gentle questions, and then said something Kiara would never forget:

"This is completely normal. The body stores waste for years. When it starts to flush it out for the first time, it takes time. It's just your body doing its job."

No medicines were prescribed.

Just rest, comfort, and the assurance that this, too, was part of growing up.

Kiara returned home that day with a new understanding—not just about her body, but about her strength. She hadn't panicked. She had gone through something unknown, alone at first, and came out of it a little quieter, a little wiser.

That first cycle lasted eighteen days, but what lasted longer was the quiet shift within her.

Childhood had started making room for something new.

And the time?

It was flying.

CHAPTER SIXTEEN

The House That Held Us

The year had passed like a whirlwind—of unexpected turns, deep changes, and quiet resilience. And finally, as winter tiptoed in with its soft breeze and the faint smell of naphthalene from packed shawls, we moved into the new home.

It was ready now.

The paint had dried, the tiles had settled, and our memories from the old flat were packed—not in boxes, but in hearts. We stood outside the door that morning, our shoes dusty from the stairs, carrying everything that truly mattered.

Dadi wasn't with us anymore.

She hadn't seen the finished home. She never stepped into the kitchen she would've surely made her own. But somehow, she was everywhere. In the way the morning light hit the dining wall. In the quiet corner beside the balcony that used to be her tea spot. In the smell of turmeric from the first sabzi cooked on the new gas stove.

We placed her photo in the living room—next to the mandir, framed in soft gold. A diya flickered beside it every morning. Kunal sometimes spoke to her like she could still hear him. Maybe... she could.

Dadu had changed in ways we didn't speak about openly. He walked slower, spoke softer. His eyes would sometimes wander off to nothing in particular. But there was strength in him too—a silent promise to keep going, for all of us. He started spending his evenings reading the newspaper aloud to Kunal, just like Dadi used to do for him.

"Let's sit by the window, the light is better," he would say. But we all knew it wasn't about the light.

The new house felt different. Bigger. Brighter. But also more grown-up.

And maybe we were growing too.

Kunal had his own school desk now and insisted on packing his bag "by himself." I had started keeping a diary, scribbling down the confusing, beautiful things happening inside me that I wasn't ready to say aloud.

Papa still left early every morning on his scooter, but now he paused at the mandir for a full minute before he stepped out. Mumma had new routines now—new walls to wipe down, new utensils to arrange, new reasons to make the same old comfort food that somehow still tasted like childhood.

On weekends, we brought the carrom board out. It still had the same old scratch marks, the same missing black coin. Kunal and I still fought over who got to be on Papa's team. Some things, it seemed, would never change.

But some things... had.

I found myself returning to certain memories more often now.

The first time Dadi taught me to roll roti edges perfectly. The night Kunal whispered ghost fears under the blanket. The smell of fresh paint when Papa showed Mumma the kitchen through the window. The sound of Dadi's laughter that Diwali evening when we lit diyas in the raw, unfinished flat.

The new home had room for all of it.

Not just furniture and people—but memories, mistakes, rituals, and rebirths.

And as I sat in the new living room one quiet evening, sipping chai with Mumma while Kunal made paper rockets in the corner and Dadu nodded off mid-news, I realized something:

Homes don't just hold families. They hold time.

They hold the way we were. The way we are becoming. And the echoes of those we've lost, who never really left.

This house...

This house held all of us.

And somewhere deep inside its walls, I knew—it always would.

Author's Note

The No Glam Show is deeply personal—not because it tells my story, but because it holds pieces of so many stories I've seen, heard, and felt over the years. While Kiara is fictional, the emotions she experiences are drawn from real life: the warmth of family, the quiet weight of expectations, the questions we're told not to ask, and the inner voice we often silence.

This book was written in fragments—between busy mornings, quiet nights, and everything in between. I didn't write it to be perfect. I wrote it to be honest.

If you saw yourself in Kiara, or someone you once knew, I hope you carry her story with you. I hope it makes you pause, reflect, and remember that even the most ordinary lives are layered with meaning.

Thank you for reading.

— Kanika Bhatia Tomar

About The Author

Kanika Bhatia Tomar is a writer and communication strategist with a background in journalism and storytelling. Her debut novel, The No Glam Show, is a deeply personal exploration of womanhood, emotional legacy, and the invisible threads that bind generations. Through both her fiction and her digital platform, ImperfectlyPerfectMaa, Kanika creates honest narratives around motherhood, identity, and the everyday moments that shape us. Her writing is defined by its emotional truth, cultural grounding, and an unwavering focus on the voices often left unheard. When she's not writing, she is navigating life as a working mother, sipping cold coffee, and documenting the beauty in life's quiet chaos.